Love Shoulda Brought You Home
A "Holy Rock Chronicles" Short

Get more Info About Shelia E. Bell books!

"Perfect Stories About Imperfect People
Like You...and Me!"

Love Shoulda Brought You Home
A "Holy Rock Chronicles" Short

Get more Info About Shelia E. Bell books!

Shelia Writes Books

Perfect Stories About Imperfect People Like You...and Me!

MULTI-AWARD WINNING
NATIONAL BESTSELLING AUTHOR
SHELIA E. BELL

ISBN: 979-8-9867834-1-3

This is a work of fiction. Any references or similarities to actual events, real people living, or dead, or to real locales are intended to give the novel a sense of reality. Any similarity in other names, characters, places, and incidents is purely coincidental

Library of Congress Control Number: 2023906554

www.sheliawritebooks.com
Aurora, Colorado

"Holy Rock Chronicles" is a spinoff series of short stories that take you on an addictive journey into the intriguing lives of the notorious members of the Graham and McCoy families from the national bestselling "My Son's Wife" series. These shorts are specially crafted to provide an exclusive, behind-the-scenes look at the characters' lives while I continue to pen the next thrilling installment in this captivating family saga. I am grateful for your continued support and for choosing to read my work.

Books 4-6
Christian Black, Esq.
If Your Price Is Right
Love Shoulda Brought You Home

one

"It's better to be healthy alone than sick with someone else." Phil McGraw

Xavier emerged from the car, his heart racing, not from anticipation but from mounting anxiety. As if on autopilot, he locked hands with his wife and strode towards the restaurant, rumored to be one of the best in the city, a place where every dish was a work of art and every sip of wine a revelation. As they walked towards the entrance, Xavier felt his sense of anxiety increasing.

This day marked three years since he and Pepper exchanged vows. He wanted to make this evening special for her, to show her how much he appreciated her unconditional love and devotion. But as he gazed around the restaurant, he felt a pang of unease. Was this really the life he had imagined for himself? A married father of two, living a so-called "normal" life? Was there a way for him to find true happiness, something more, something beyond the confines of his current situation?

Despite his deep love for his two-year-old sons, Zavion and Davion, Xavier couldn't shake the feeling that something was missing. Still, he put on a brave face and followed the hostess toward their reserved table.

As they were led through the elegant foyer and into the dining room, Xavier temporarily pushed aside his anxiety and became impressed by the sheer beauty of the place. The tables were set with crisp white linens, polished silverware, and sparkling crystal glasses, and the whole room seemed to glow with a transcendent radiance.

Pepper's smile grew wider as they arrived at their table. Xavier forced himself to match her enthusiasm.

"Zay, I see why this place is supposed to be on the same level as some of the Michelin-star restaurants," Pepper said, smiling big as they were seated.

"Yes, it *is* nice," Xavier agreed. It took every ounce of mental fortitude to keep a smile on his face.

†

"This food is divine," Pepper complimented, taking another big bite of her juicy and tender New York strip. "What a way to celebrate three years of marriage. You can be so romantic and thoughtful." Pepper reached over the table and grabbed his hand, gently kneading it. "I love you. Thank you for sticking it out. I know I went to a dark place after the babies were born. I wish I could have done something to change that."

"It wasn't your fault," Xavier spoke up, switching her hand to his. "It happens to women more than you think. I learned that when you were diagnosed."

"Postpartum psychosis. Who would have thought it would happen to me."

"Look, don't go down that road. We're here to have a good time, get some free time away from the boys, and well—"

"Celebrate our love. Let's toast," Pepper added and raised her glass of white wine.

Xavier met her glass in the air with his.

"To not just three, but a lifetime of sheer love and happiness with you, Zay!" Her eyes sparkled with anticipation as she giggled and playfully covered her mouth with her hand.

Xavier's heart raced. His fingers tightened around the stem of his glass. He felt like a wild animal ready to pounce. His breaths were short, and his pulse pounded in his ears. His gaze fixed, a smile that seemed unnatural pulled at the edges of his mouth. He was like a coiled spring, ready to unleash a flood of emotions that would shake the very foundation of his world. He was well aware that he was on the edge of what he could only describe as a point of no return. But he was ready to take the leap. He couldn't keep on this way. It wasn't fair to him and it certainly wasn't fair to the woman sitting across the table from him. Yes, the time had come for him to rise up and take control of his destiny, no matter the cost.

two

"If you can't figure out where you stand with someone, it might be time to stop standing and start walking." Unknown

"Thanks for a wonderful evening." Pepper wrapped her arms around Xavier, and pulled herself up to snuggle in closer, hoping to reignite the passion that once flowed effortlessly between them. She had always been the initiator in their relationship; more often than not, Xavier met her advances with eager enthusiasm. But lately, something had shifted.

Tonight, despite her best efforts to arouse him, he remained unresponsive, and she couldn't help but feel a sense of desperation wash over her. She could feel the tension in his body, the way he stiffened against her touch as if he was repulsed by her very presence.

"Pepper, not tonight," he uttered, firmly pushing her off his chest, leaving no room for argument.

With a defeated sigh, Pepper fell back on the bed, her face twisted in a pout of frustration and anger. It had been weeks since they made love. She hoped tonight, their anniversary, things would be different. But she knew him all too well—this was the side of him that didn't crave her touch, that didn't hunger for her scent, that didn't ache for her. It was a side of him that yearned for something beyond her grasp, something she could never satisfy. It was like an unpredictable storm that raged within him, sometimes calm and sometimes turbulent. But this time, it was different. It was more intense, more powerful. She could feel it, sense it, see it.

As she held onto him tightly, she couldn't help but wonder if this was the beginning of the end. The fear of losing him was like a raging fire within her, and she was powerless to extinguish it.

She shifted herself into an upright position on the bed, her eyes scanning his face. "All right, what's the matter?" she asked, as if she didn't already know. She folded her arms and rested her back against the headboard.

"I'm not sure what you mean," he responded, the hint of annoyance creeping into his tone.

You're what, Zay? Tired of your family? Tired of this life? Or are you just tired of me? Tell me, what's bothering you?"

Her words struck like lightning, cutting through the tension that had been building up between them for only God knew how long.

Xavier clenched his jaw, his eyes dark with emotions he was struggling to contain. "I'm not tired of this life," he began, his voice low and intense. "I'm tired of living it for everyone else. My father's in prison, and I'm expected to stay at New Holy Rock with Uncle Stiles and help keep the church afloat when I want no part of it. I've never been able to do me. It's always the family this and the family that. It feels like I'm in prison myself. Well, I'm not that guy. I never have been and I never wanted to be. Then there's...you—" he stopped.

"Don't stop now. What about me?" Pepper puffed up.

"It's like you never give me a moment to breathe." He paused, taking a deep breath. "I've been holding this in too long. From the moment I met you, it's been all or nothing with you. Don't get me wrong; I mean, you couldn't manipulate and attach yourself to me unless I allowed it. But I'm tired of pretending like all is well. What about me? What about what I want, what I need? It's like you can't see past yourself."

His words hung heavy in the air, the tension between them now at its breaking point. Xavier's eyes never left hers, his expression raw and unguarded. He was done pretending, done playing the part of the dutiful husband. It was time for the truth, no matter how painful it might be.

"Don't you dare make this my fault!" Pepper's voice thundered through the room, full of pent-up frustration and anger of her own.

"Dang it," he shot back, his eyes flashing with intensity. "You knew who I was when you met me! But you wouldn't back off. You just kept on and on poking and prodding until I...until I just said what the heck and pretended I could live this life. Well, you got me, Pepper. You wanted the thrill, the danger, the rush. But you didn't think about the consequences. As for me, I can't keep pretending. I can't keep acting like I'm this happily married man with wonderful kids and a beautiful wife and life. I'm grateful for my sons, but this life right here..." He looked around their bedroom.

His fists clenched, and in one swift motion, he sprang off the bed, his heart pounding with adrenaline as he paced back and forth across the room. His thoughts raced, his emotions on the edge, and he knew he had to get out of there before he did or said something he'd regret. The tension in the air was electric, and it was all he could do to keep from exploding.

Pepper recoiled. His words hit her like a slap in the face, leaving her breathless and reeling. Her mind was racing with a million thoughts and emotions, each one more intense than the last.

three

"The hardest thing you can do is to let go of someone you love when you know it would be best for them and for you." Unknown

One week after their anniversary, Pepper stood frozen in the doorway, her heart pounding in her chest as Zavion and Davion clung to her legs, their small hands gripping her jeans tightly. She could feel the weight of their fear and confusion, and it threatened to drag her down.

She took a deep breath and steadied herself, leaning against the wall in the foyer as Xavier approached pulling a metallic suitcase on wheels, his face a mask of determination as he strode toward them.

Pepper could feel the tension in the air, the unspoken words hanging between them like a heavy fog. She knew that this was it, the moment that would change everything.

Xavier's eyes met hers. She thought she saw a flash of sadness and regret in his gaze. Maybe it was just her imagination. He wore a black backpack over one shoulder, his posture stiff and resolute as he came to a stop in front of her.

For a moment, neither of them spoke. The only sound was the whimpering of the children clinging to her legs.

And then, with a suddenness that took her breath away, Xavier spoke. "I need to get away. I don't know how long I'll be gone," he said, his voice calm but deliberate.

"What does that equate to, Xavier? You're going to have to do better than that. Are you talking about a day, two days, a week? What?" Pepper felt a surge of panic rise in her chest, but she told herself to stay calm.

Xavier's gaze flickered down to the boys at her feet, his expression softening as he took in their sweet innocent faces. Without hesitation, he knelt down and pulled them both into a tight embrace.

Pepper felt her heart swell with emotion as she watched them, the scene playing out before her like a bittersweet symphony. She could see the love and tenderness in Xavier's eyes as he kissed each of the boys on the cheek, his fingers ruffling their thick black hair.

For a moment, the world around them seemed to fall away, leaving only the four of them in a bubble of warmth and affection. And then, with a heavy sigh, Xavier rose to his feet, his gaze meeting hers once again.

"I'm sorry," he said, his voice thick with emotion. "I'm so sorry for all of this. Just give me some time. That's all I'm asking. I need to clear my head so I can be a better father to the boys and a better husband to you."

"But you can do that here. I don't see why you have to leave, Zay," Pepper cried, trying to shield her tears from their sons.

"See, that's what I'm talking about. You just don't get it." He felt himself growing frustrated. Pepper could have that effect on him. It was why he knew he could never work things out in his head as long as he was staying under the same roof with her or the same city for that matter.

"I can't do this!" he emphasized. "I need time to think, to get *me* together. I can't do that being here. I need to find myself again," he uttered through clenched teeth. His movements were quick and precise. He kissed her on the cheek, then opened the door.

Pepper felt a lump rise in her throat as she watched him go, the suitcase trailing behind him like a shadow. Tears rolled down her cheeks as the weight of his words settled heavily in her heart. For a moment, she was frozen in place, unsure of what to do. Was this goodbye? Was the life they had built together over? She felt it in her gut and saw it on Xavier's face. And then, with a sudden clarity, she knew. She had to let him go. It was the only way.

four

"A healthy relationship will never require you to sacrifice your happiness, your goals, or your friends." Mandy Hale

After breezing through TSA, Xavier made his way to his gate, passing an Apple® store on the way. Something inside him stirred, and before he knew it, he impulsively walked in. With at least an hour to kill before boarding, he had time to spare. When he emerged, he had erased all data on his phone, disconnected his service, and left the store phoneless. The weight of his actions settled on him like a heavy blanket.

Walking to his gate, his mind whirled with conflicting emotions. Yet, with each step he took, he felt a sense of clarity and purpose. Discarding his phone was just the beginning; he knew he had many more things to let go of in order to embrace whatever lay ahead.

Settling into his seat in the luxurious comfort of business class, Xavier let out a deep sigh and closed his eyes, savoring the feeling of freedom that came with his decision. No return ticket, no set plans. He would discover whatever was ahead for him when he arrived in Portland, Oregon. The possibilities were endless, and he was ready to embrace them all.

He chose Oregon because it was known to be more liberal. In high school, he visited the Oregon coast on a senior class trip. He loved it back then.

However, this was his first time spending any time in the city of Portland. But he believed this could very well be the place where he could rediscover himself and find out what path he wanted to travel.

As if on cue, a strikingly handsome flight attendant approached him with a warm smile, his long blond hair cascading down his olive-toned face in soft waves. "Is there anything I can offer you, sir?" he asked, his voice smooth and soothing. "Perhaps some refreshing water, a hot cup of tea, or a cup of coffee? Or, if you're feeling a bit adventurous, something a bit stronger?" the attendant subtly flirted.

Xavier felt a twinge of excitement at the offer of something stronger. He glanced up at the flight attendant, his eyes gleaming with anticipation.

"Surprise me," Xavier said with a flirty grin. "Oh, would you mind getting me a blanket and pillow as well?" Xavier requested, feeling a slight chill in the cabin.

"Absolutely," the attentive flight attendant replied with a gracious smile. He swiftly retrieved a plush blanket and a small but fluffy pillow from an overhead bin, presenting them to Xavier before retreating to attend to other passengers.

In no time, he was back at Xavier's side, with a glass of rich amber-colored liquor, and a glass of ice.

"On the house," he murmured, along with a smile and a wink.

"Thank you," Xavier replied with a smile, settling deeper into his seat while savoring the taste of the smooth liquor.

Xavier thought about where he would go and what he would do when he arrived in the City of Roses. Pulling the blanket up to his shoulders and the pillow behind his neck, he fully relaxed. For a brief moment, he allowed his mind to go back to the scene with Pepper and the boys. He quickly replaced those troubling thoughts by opening his wallet and retrieving the printout with his hotel information. He had reserved a corner suite at a luxury hotel, with a stunning view of the Willamette River. It wasn't exactly cheap, but spending money was the least of his concerns. Being the financial wizard he'd always been, he had accumulated a hefty nest egg for his wife and kids, and unknown to Pepper he had also put aside more than enough to make life comfortable for himself.

Upon entering his hotel suite later that evening, he was immediately impressed by the elegant decoration that featured modern furnishings and a neutral color palette. It fit his taste to a tee.

In a separate space from the living room was the bedroom. As he entered, Xavier parked his suitcase in the corner and flung his backpack on top of it. He was relieved to see a king-sized bed and an en-suite bathroom.

After taking a shower, he dressed in the soft plush white robe, compliments of the hotel. He made himself a cup of hot apple cider tea and stood in front of the stunning floor-to-ceiling windows showcasing the Willamette River. This was his time and he was going to take advantage of every single moment. After all, tomorrow was not promised.

five

"Worry never robs tomorrow of its sorrow, it only saps today of its joy." Leo Buscaglia

It had been three and a half days since Xavier left home. Pepper called and texted him relentlessly, desperate for any sign that he was okay. No response. He hadn't even checked on their boys, making her heart ache with worry. Her worry grew into an all-consuming fear when she called him this last time and his phone was no longer in service.

Tears streaming down her face, Pepper poured out her fears to Eliana as they walked through City Park with their kids. Being the First Lady of Holy Rock, Eliana believed it was her duty and responsibility to always be ready with a listening ear and a comforting word. She prayed for the McCoy family, especially Pepper. As their friendship blossomed, Eliana went above and beyond to support Pepper through her struggles.

Pepper found Eliana to be a reliable source of comfort and someone easy to talk to.

"Everything is going to be fine. Trust God," Eliana said, stopping along the walking trail to embrace Pepper. "Think about it. Khalil hasn't said anything about Xavier lately, which to me means Xavier must be okay. He would have told me if he heard anything different," Eliana said, trying to reassure her friend. "Don't get me wrong, I know how Khalil can have tunnel vision where he doesn't worry about anything or anybody unless it directly affects him."

"Exactly, which is why I don't see Xavier reaching out to Khalil, not unless he was in deep trouble. I know they're brothers, but you and I both know they're not as close as some brothers."

"Exactly, which means no news is good news," said Eliana.

Even with Eliana's comforting words, Pepper couldn't shake the feeling that something was seriously wrong. Her frustration boiled over as she threw up her hands in despair.

"But no phone calls or texts? And now his phone is off? Don't you think that's enough to warrant me worrying about my husband? I don't know where he is. Heck, he could still be in the city somewhere with somebody else for all I know! God, please just let him be okay."

The thought made her stomach churn with anxiety. She didn't see Xavier as the type of father who would run out on his sons, but what if he was? The suspense was killing her, and she couldn't help but fear the worst.

"Girl, please. I don't believe Xavier is still in Memphis. You know better than that. No way would that man be in the city and not have any contact with his sons."

"He's somewhere out there. Only God knows where," Pepper lamented.

†

Xavier's footsteps echoed against the cobblestoned sidewalks of downtown Portland. The warm glow of the sun setting over the horizon highlighted the historical landmarks and small businesses surrounding him. He passed people sitting on benches and others talking and dining at outdoor tables. The streets were illuminated by the glow of streetlights and neon signs.

As he continued his walk, he came upon a bakery. The tantalizing scent of freshly-baked pastries and rich coffee hung thick in the air, enveloping him in a momentary cocoon of serenity, and he felt an inexplicable urge to go inside.

Perching himself at a window seat, he gazed out at the world beyond. Xavier felt a sense of urgency gnawing at his soul. His life felt stagnant, unfulfilling, and he had no one to turn to. His loneliness was suffocating, driving him to desperate measures. He reached out to his long-lost love, Ian. But the hope he clung to was quickly shattered once again when he heard the usual automated message.

His mind began racing with thoughts of the past, questioning every choice he had ever made, every path he had taken. He realized he would never be himself as long as he was married to Pepper. He had sacrificed his happiness for the sake of his children, staying with her even though he knew he could never truly love her.

Xavier was broken and unfulfilled. He told himself that he could never give his boys the love they deserved until he found it himself. Guilt weighed heavily on his chest like a crushing weight that threatened to engulf him. Yet, he knew he couldn't put all the blame on Pepper. She was a wonderful human being, deserving of nothing less than a love that was whole-hearted and true. The half-hearted, lackluster affection that he had given her in the past was simply not enough. She had to see that he wasn't capable of loving her unconditionally, not in the way a man would truly love a woman like her. He wasn't that man and never would be. Why couldn't she see that as clearly as he saw it?

Without giving it thought, he pulled out his new over-the-counter flip phone and tapped out a message to Pepper. It wasn't fair for him to leave and not at least let her know that he was okay. It was bad enough that he didn't tell her where he was going or when he would be back. She was probably suffering in silence, afraid to tell her mother that he'd walked out on her and the boys. She could be like that, wanting people to believe her life was perfect and happy when in reality Xavier looked at it as a total disaster.

He read the text message slowly and then paused a second or two before pressing DELETE.

six

"It's not always tears that measure the pain.
Sometimes it's the smile we fake." Unknown

Xavier had been in Portland for almost two weeks. He wandered the crowded streets of Triangle Hill, the heart of Portland's gay hub scene, randomly and unintentionally bumping into people, peeking in at various bars and restaurants along the way. Streams of light lined the rain-soaked sidewalks, making his shadow loom larger than normal. Shoulders hunched, hands in pockets, head hanging, he trudged along the strip like it was a familiar part of his life. With his earbuds in his ears, much of the sounds of a busy Friday evening went unheard and unnoticed.

"Hey, watch out," someone said.

"Sorry," Xavier mumbled as he pulled one earbud out of his ear and looked over his shoulder as a purple-haired guy skateboarded past.

A neon rainbow sign hanging outside a popular gay bar beckoned Xavier, inviting him into the welcoming environment. As he walked through the dimly lit bar, he took in the eclectic decor. It had a laid-back atmosphere that made Xavier feel at ease as he sipped on a beer. A string of dartboards, pool tables, and sports games in the back of the bar provided low-key entertainment, while the friendly staff and welcoming atmosphere made him feel at ease.

As the night wore on, several men approached him displaying varying degrees of interest. But Xavier wasn't ready for anything serious, and he spent the night warding off their advances while indulging in more beers. He left that bar and meandered around Triangle Hill, indulging in more beers at other pubs while warding off advances from more strangers.

Later that evening, sitting on the balcony of his hotel suite, Xavier took several shots of vodka while gazing out at the peaceful harbor. The alcohol was a departure from his usual fruity drinks, but he needed something stronger to soothe his troubled mind. Drinking beer, like he had done tonight, wasn't normal for him either, yet he had more than his fair share of that too. A lot of things he'd done in his twenty-something-year-old life probably weren't normal, including his marriage.

Tonight, he was in his feelings so he chose something other than beer to nurse his emotional wounds. But the liquor brought no peace. Instead, he was overcome by thoughts of inadequacy and guilt. He had a beautiful wife and kids in Memphis who loved him, and a good position making a substantial salary at his father's church, yet he felt like a hypocrite, unsure of what he truly had to offer.

†

The next morning, Xavier woke up in a daze, half-naked on the oversized sofa with two empty bottles of vodka strewn across the floor. His head pounded as if a marching band were performing inside his skull.

Xavier forced himself to sit up, his body feeling heavy and sluggish, but he slowly rose to his feet and dragged himself into the bedroom. But as soon as he darted the door, his eyes widened in shock at the sight before him—someone was asleep in his bed. Xavier's heart began to pound in his chest as he cautiously approached the stranger. The man was sprawled out on the bed, snoring softly, oblivious to Xavier's presence. Xavier's mind raced, as he tried to piece together the events of the previous night. Had he invited this man into his hotel room? And if so, what happened between them?

As Xavier stood there, staring at the stranger, the man stirred and slowly opened his eyes. He looked up at Xavier, a sleepy smile spreading across his face.

"Hey there, handsome," the stranger said, his voice deep and husky.

Xavier's heart skipped a beat as he realized that this man was not just a stranger, but a man he met at the downstairs hotel bar the night before, or so he remembered. He must have invited the man to his room with the intention of doing only God knows what. He felt a flush of embarrassment wash over him as he realized what he had done.

"Who are you?" Xavier asked, his voice shaky.

The piercing blue-eyed man sat up in the bed, stretched his arms above his head, and pushed his shiny straight black hair off his face. "Name's

Connor. And I must tell you that you, my friend, are one hell of a good time."

Xavier shook his head, trying to clear the fog from his mind. "I don't remember bringing you back here."

With a look of delight, Connor let out a laugh. "Yeah, well, you were pretty wasted. But don't worry, I won't hold it against you."

Xavier's stomach churned until he became nauseated with a mixture of disgust, anxiety, and regret. He didn't remember anything from the night before. What had he done? What else had he forgotten?

"Did we?" Xavier asked, looking away in embarrassment.

Connor laughed. "You really have to ask?"

"You need to leave," Xavier said firmly. "Now."

Despite Xavier's clear discomfort, Connor seemed to be enjoying the situation, taking his time to get dressed and continuing to flirt.

The more Connor talked, the more Xavier felt his control slipping, overwhelmed by his own carelessness.

Finally, Connor made his way to the door, but not before placing his business card into Xavier's hand. "Call me if you want to have some more fun," he said with a sly grin. "I'm in town until Monday."

"Wait," Xavier said, his heart pounding in his chest.

Connor turned around, his eyes full of amusement. "What is it, my friend?"

"Did we...uhh, use protection?" Xavier asked, his voice shaking with fear.

"Protection?" Connor laughed, the sound of his shrill laughter ringing through the room. "Why would we need protection? Anyway, no need to worry about that, my friend," he said, dismissing Xavier's concerns without a second thought. "See you around." And with that, he was gone, leaving Xavier to grapple with the aftermath of their reckless encounter.

As soon as Connor stepped into the corridor, Xavier's reflexes kicked in and he slammed the door shut with a loud thud. Overwhelmed by a sense of panic and disgust, he stumbled towards the bathroom and stared at himself in the mirror. The sight of his disheveled appearance only served to aggravate his already jumbled state of mind.

He couldn't believe how far he had fallen. His life seemed to be careening out of control at an alarming rate, leaving him grasping for something, anything, to hold onto. With each passing moment, he felt himself slipping further and further away from the person he once was.

As he stared at his reflection, he wondered how much more he could take before completely losing himself. It was a scary thought, one that left him feeling more alone than ever before.

seven

"It hurts to let go, but sometimes it hurts more to hold on." Unknown

Xavier walked along the busy downtown sidewalks. The stark contrast between the daytime crowds and the nighttime scene was evident. What was he doing and why had he behaved so recklessly? He replayed the events from a couple of nights ago over and over in his mind but he still couldn't recall inviting the guy who said his name was Connor into his hotel suite. Obviously, that's exactly what happened.

He stopped at a deli. Shifting his focus as he ate, his mind wandered to his family, specifically Pepper, and their children. Leaving his boys and abandoning his responsibilities was not something he took lightly, but he couldn't continue living a lie. He had always been the one to fix things, to be the hero, but at what cost?

Xavier was all too aware that Pepper would eventually spill the beans to her mother and Fancy about him leaving if she hadn't done so already. However, she could be a private person when it came to discussing the intimate details of her marriage. As such, there was a chance the women might still be in the dark about his hasty exit.

As for Stiles, Hezekiah, and Khalil and their feelings about his life choices, Xavier hadn't given them much thought. Hezekiah made it clear years ago when Xavier was a teen, that he was displeased with his son's preferred lifestyle. They had since patched their relationship, but there was still a separation. His Uncle Stiles didn't say much, if anything about it. Khalil, much like Hezekiah, didn't like the fact he was gay. Xavier believed it was the reason he and his brother were not close as Xavier desired. His family would never be able to understand what he was going through, what he was wrestling with. Heck, he had no idea what he was dealing with either. What was he going to do? One thing he was sure of, he wasn't ready to return home and pretend like everything was okay.

The last message he had exchanged with his mother was a few days before he left Memphis. Thinking about it, he realized their conversation had been nothing more than a courteous exchange of words. There was no hint of the turbulent storm that was brewing in his life, and he couldn't help but feel a twinge of guilt for keeping his plans a secret from his family, particularly his mother.

Despite the enormity of his decision, Xavier felt a sense of liberation knowing that he had sufficient cash at his disposal, providing him with enough cushion to maintain his lifestyle for some time, depending on his spending habits.

He had stuck with Pepper for the past three years, even convinced himself that his physical attraction to her meant he was *straight*, but that test had failed miserably. He was stuck in a life of misery unless he made a drastic change.

Xavier's internal struggles were compounded by the fact that he had never been truly in love with Pepper. The weight of his demons threatened to crush him, but he knew that he couldn't keep living a lie. Would his departure ultimately bring peace to his loved ones or just to him?

With a sense of purpose, he settled his bill and left the deli, heading towards other hotels and Airbnbs he had researched online. He was determined to find the perfect place that would satisfy his budget and preferences, a base from which he could plot his next move.

eight

"Love shoulda brought you home last night." Toni
Braxton

"If he loved his kids like he says he does. And if
he loves me even a little bit, then love shoulda
brought him home. But he's been gone for two
freaking weeks and not a word, Khalil. Where could
he be? And why in the heck is his phone
disconnected?" Pepper cried, pacing across the
carpeted floor in Khalil's office.

Khalil walked up to her and pulled her into a
comforting embrace, his words gentle and soothing.
"Take a deep breath. We'll find him. My brother can
take care of himself," he assured her, hoping to
calm her visibly anxious state.

Pepper's worried eyes darted back and forth.
"He's never done anything like this before. He
always tells me where he's going and when he'll be
back."

Suddenly, her phone beeped, and she gasped as
she read the message. "It's him, Khalil. It's Zay!"

Reading the message aloud, Pepper's voice
trembled with fear. "I know you must be worried. don't
be. I'm straight. Give the boys a hug and kiss from me.
Talk to you soon. Zay. " The message only increased
her worry.

As she studied the unknown number, a wave of apprehension washed over her. "Whose number is this? It's not his," she said, her voice quivering.

Khalil strode over to his desk and sank into his chair, his brow furrowed with contemplation. "Maybe it's a replacement phone. You said his phone had been disconnected. That could be because he lost it or broke it or something. That's probably a new number they gave him. That could be why you haven't heard from him until now. Please, sit down, Pepper. Take a minute to calm down."

Pepper wiped away her tears with the back of her hand. "I don't want to sit down and I won't calm down. My husband is missing, and I don't know where he is. I want him home. We need him home. The boys miss him. They ask about their daddy constantly, and I don't know what to tell them other than he'll be back soon. But I don't know if he *will* be back," she said, her voice breaking.

Khalil leaned back in his chair, his expression thoughtful. "He'll be back. You and I both know he's been struggling with a lot. Trying to live a Godly life while dealing with his inner demons, particularly his sexuality. It's tough. To be honest, my brother has always been sensitive about his homosexuality. I don't know how he's managed to stay in this marriage for three years. I'm not trying to be mean, but him marrying a straight woman like you has always been confusing to me."

Pepper's eyes narrowed as she glared at Khalil. "Are you suggesting that I'm to blame for Xavier's

27

disappearance?" she spat, her voice filled with frustration and anger.

Khalil shook his head quickly, trying to defuse the tension. "No, that's not what I meant. It's just that him getting married to a woman was unexpected, a surprise that's all."

"Well, it shouldn't be," Pepper retorted. "Xavier and I love each other, and we have a family together. That should be all that matters." Pepper's hands were shaking with emotion. "I can't believe this. I thought you were on our side, Khalil."

Khalil leaned forward, his expression serious. "Look, I'm not trying to diminish your marriage, Pepper. I just know how much my brother has struggled over the years. It's no secret that I've always been open about my feelings on the matter. So it was just surprising to hear he had gotten married to a woman."

Pepper's face fell as she thought about Xavier's past struggles. "I know he's had a hard time, but you have to believe me when I say we love each other. And he's always been honest with me about everything."

Khalil let out a deep sigh and ran a hand through his hair. "I'm sorry, I didn't mean to upset you," he said, his voice laced with remorse. Rising from his chair, he made his way over to her.

"I should probably get going. I promised the sitter I wouldn't be away long," she said, turning away from him and heading towards the door.

"Sure, well give my nephews a hug from their Uncle Khalil. I'll stop by and see them soon. Oh, by the way, Eliana may call you to arrange a playdate for Khaliyah and the boys," he said, steering the conversation to a more cheerful topic.

Pepper nodded solemnly, her heart weighing heavily. "Okay. And Khalil—"

"Yes?"

Thanks for your concern," she said softly but then hesitated before continuing. "But I want to make it clear that Xavier marrying me was entirely out of love. It had nothing to do with any sort of pressure or obligation," she stated firmly.

With that, she swiftly departed, driven by a fierce resolve to demonstrate to Khalil, and anyone else who questioned the authenticity of her relationship, that she and Xavier were destined to be together.

nine

*"The worst feeling in the world is knowing you did
the best you could and it still wasn't enough."*
Unknown

Fancy and Victoria huddled around the family
dining table, their hearts heavy with concern. The
room was tense, as Pepper sat at the head of the
table, tears streaming down her face. Earlier that
day, Victoria had come over to find her daughter in
the kitchen, her sobs echoing throughout the
house. It was clear that something was wrong.

With heavy hearts, Pepper revealed the awful
news that Xavier had left town, leaving his family
behind. Victoria was stunned. Right away, she
knew that she had to do something to help her
daughter. Without hesitation, she phoned Fancy.

Less than half an hour later Fancy arrived. The
two women gathered around Pepper, offering words
of comfort and support. Despite their best efforts,
Pepper was practically inconsolable. She couldn't
understand why Xavier would leave his family
behind, especially his two young sons.

"I should have known something was going on
with him. I haven't talked to him or seen him in a
few weeks. I thought it was because he was busy,
he always is, but for you to say he just up and left.
What has gotten into him? And you say y'all didn't
have a fight. Was he worried about something we

didn't know about? What could it be?" questioned Fancy.

"What did he say the last time you spoke?" Victoria asked Fancy.

Fancy frowned. "Nothing that would lead me to think he was about to walk out on his family. Just regular talk."

"He's been gone for two weeks," Pepper repeated, a fresh batch of tears pouring down her face like a runaway river. "And, no, we didn't have a fight. I told you, we had just celebrated our third wedding anniversary. Everything was so special. Then like Hulk, he flipped."

With determination etched on her face, Fancy spoke up, "We're going to find him, one way or another. I need to call Khalil."

"Khalil already knows. I told him," Pepper said.

Victoria offered her own words of hope and encouragement. "You said he asked that you give him some time because he needed to clear his head. Right?"

"Yes, but it still doesn't make sense. Why did he have to leave to clear his head, and why won't he tell me where he is? There's so much that just doesn't make sense. Oh, God, please don't let him be in trouble. Let him be okay," Pepper cried.

Victoria got up from the island stool and went over and embraced her daughter. "Shhh, it's going to be all right. He'll be home before you know it."

"We have to have faith. Anyway, there's no proof that he's in any danger. Knowing my son, he's probably checked into a hotel right here in the city somewhere. We know he wouldn't leave those boys like some deadbeat."

"Speaking of the boys, I'll go check on them. Hopefully, they're still napping."

"No need, you can see them right there. They're still asleep. See—" Pepper pointed to a baby monitor sitting on a countertop at the opposite side of the oversized kitchen.

"I keep forgetting about that monitor," Victoria said, smiling as she walked over to the monitor and gazed at her grandsons asleep in their toddler beds.

"Good, let's hope they keep napping for a bit longer. Either way, I'll be here when they wake up. If you want me to, I'll stay tonight or for as long as you need me," Fancy offered. "Victoria, I know you have work tomorrow, so don't worry. I have everything under control."

"Thanks, Fancy," Pepper murmured. "But please don't feel like you have to."

"Fancy, that's a good idea. Why don't I spend the night too? Would you like that, sweetheart?" Victoria asked Pepper who appeared to be slowly calming down.

"Yes, but I told y'all, I don't want to be a burden. Me and the boys will be fine. Plus, I can always call our sitter."

"No, we've got this. Now why don't you go and take a nap? We can go pick up a change of clothes later. You look like you haven't had a moment's rest," said Fancy, ambling over to Pepper and patting her on the back.

"Yeah, I haven't been able to sleep much since Xavier left."

"Fancy's right, why don't you go to your room? Get some rest. We'll see to the boys when they wake up," said Victoria.

"In the meantime, I'll make some phone calls and see what I can find out, if anything, about where Xavier might have gone."

Fancy jumped into action, and started making phone calls and scouring the internet for any information she could find about her son's possible whereabouts, keeping faith that they would find him.

ten

"Heartbreak is a loss unlike any other." Stephanie
Ericsson

Seventeen days had passed since Xavier's
sudden departure from Memphis, a decision he
had arrived at after much consideration, despite
the difficulty it presented in leaving behind his wife
and children. If he wanted to make something of
his life for himself, he saw leaving as being the only
viable option. Despite his best efforts, his marriage
was not thriving, and he realized he could not
imagine spending a lifetime with Pepper or any
woman. After three years of struggling, he had
come to terms with the fact that his current
situation was unbearable.

The call he recently made to Pepper from his
new phone was successful, and he was glad he had
made the decision to turn off his iPhone and
purchase this phone, but hearing Pepper's voice
and the boys in the background, gave him pause.
He found himself thinking of them constantly. He
never wanted his boys to think he had abandoned
them. *But isn't that what I've done?* he questioned
himself.

He imagined Pepper telling his mother, and
everyone close to him, that he had left her.
Knowing his mother as he did, he could see Fancy
running around doing everything possible to find
him and make him come back home. But that part
of his life, of being controlled, manipulated, and

told what to do, how to live, and who he should love was over. It was time he stood up for himself even if that meant someone else might get hurt in the process. He would never intentionally hurt another person, but at this stage of his life, it was either save himself or be miserable for the rest of his life.

"I'll reach out again when I'm ready," Xavier said aloud, his voice laced with exasperation. He ordered a light meal through room service while he continued contemplating what his next move should be.

Days after his shameful night with Connor, he had decided it was time for him to leave his hotel and find another spot. He needed a space that offered both comfort and affordability.

He stumbled upon a two-bedroom townhome on Airbnb that seemed to call out to him. The modest price tag and cozy atmosphere were just what he needed to truly embrace his solo journey.

This is it, he thought as he stepped inside the modern furnished living room. As he settled into his new surroundings, he had a feeling that his life would never be the same. It was time to break free from the expectations of others and march to the beat of his own drum. He didn't know exactly what that would entail but anything to escape the hollow emptiness and sense of loss he felt is what he needed.

He made himself comfortable on a colorful recliner before taking out his flip phone and researching social media to see if he could find any information on Ian. Eliana had refused to divulge

Ian's whereabouts and Xavier had long since stopped asking her. If she would have simply told him where her twin brother was, then all Xavier wanted to do was reach out to Ian and let him know that he had left his marriage. He didn't expect Ian to welcome him back into his life with open arms, but he did hope and pray they could at least be friends and rekindle what Xavier had thrown away.

eleven

"Heartbreak could be lived with if it weren't accompanied by regret." Laura Kasischke

Pepper took the boys to Eliana's house for a playdate with Khaliyah, hoping the time away from the house would make her feel better mentally. Times like this is when she sometimes wished she was still working rather than being a stay-at-home mom. It would keep her mind off of her present circumstances.

"I'm going to tell you what the devil hates but God loves, and that's the truth. I don't know why you keep holding on and praying for a marriage that's dead, Pepper. What are you thinking?"

"You don't understand. I believe marriage should be forever, not like my parents or other folks I've seen who got divorced. I don't want to give up, Eliana. And what you, and my mother, fail to understand is I love Xavier."

"Girl, you need to start thinking. This is not a marriage, not a real marriage anyway. It never has been. Xavier is who he is. I don't think you or anyone else can change that."

"What about Ian?" whispered Pepper.

"Did you say, what about Ian?" Elaina responded. "How many times have you asked me about my brother?"

Pepper nodded. "Have you, have you asked Ian if he's talked to Xavier?"

"I already told you, I'm not going to ask him again. He said he hasn't talked to him and he doesn't want to hear from him. Ian has moved on with his life, Pepper. He's in a relationship and he's happy. He changed his number a long time ago and he's blocked Xavier from his social media accounts. So move on from that thought of him and Xavier hooking up again."

Eliana stopped talking briefly and looked at the kids as they played in the backyard laced with toys. They were having a blast. Khaliyah was a year younger than Zavion and Davion but they played beautifully without hardly any fuss.

Zavion and Davion were already behaving like little gentlemen. They looked out for Khaliyah like she was their little sister, giving in to her every want. It was such a lovely sight for the two mothers to see.

"They're such good little boys. Look how gentle they are with Khaliyah." Eliana smiled, watching the kids.

Pepper grinned. "Thanks. I'm so blessed to have them. I thank God for healing my mind so I could be here for them. To be honest, if it wasn't for them, I don't know how I would get through one day after the next. I keep thinking about Xavier and wondering where he could be. It's killing me."

"See, that's what I'm talking about. You've got to stop it. I know you love him, but then again, do you?"

Pepper eyed her friend strangely. "What are you talking about? Of course, I love my husband. You want me to fall out of love with the father of my children?" she asked, looking at her boys playing.

"You may hate me for saying this, and if you do then I still won't apologize because you and I have become friends, and I don't like to see my friends hurt or upset. Xavier is wrong but he isn't in this alone. I think you've been fooling yourself since the very beginning. I don't know why you settled for a man who clearly is attracted to other men. He never made that a secret, Pepper. It's not like you entered this relationship or marriage blindfolded. For goodness sake, accept the truth! The man is gay! To make matters worse, he was, or still might be, in love with my twin brother! Now, don't get me wrong, I know you say he's a good father and that's great. But what about your needs, Pepper? When are you going to wake up and smell the roses, coffee, or whatever? When are you going to put yourself first?"

Pepper began to cry, but quickly stood and walked over to a nearby patio table where she picked up some napkins, using one to wipe her tears. The last thing she wanted was for her sons to see her crying. They'd witnessed enough of that since Xavier left. It wasn't good for them to see her like this so she quickly pulled herself together and returned to sit next to Eliana. The boys didn't seem to notice her actions and Pepper released a sigh of relief.

"I don't know why I married him. You're right; I knew he was gay. I guess I thought I could change him. I can't say what I was thinking. I mean, Xavier is a good man. I picked up on that from the start.

He adores his sons. He treats me like gold, and there's nothing he wouldn't do for us. When I went through that psychotic episode after giving birth, it was Xavier who took care of the boys and made sure they were good."

"Yes, but even then, think about it, Pepper. He moved my brother in with him. They were playing house like they were the ones married instead of you and Xavier. You should have been the one living in your house, not Ian! Dang, don't you see that?"

"At the time, no, I didn't see it. I was sick, Eliana," Pepper shouted back, causing all three kids to stop playing and look.

Davion ran up to his mother and stood between her legs.

"It's okay, baby. Mommy's good," she assured the toddler.

Zavion came up behind him and squeezed between her legs too. She hugged each of the boys and tussled their heads of thick, chocolate brown hair. Leaning down, she kissed each of them.

"It's okay, go back and play," she told them.

The boys ran back out in the yard and started playing again.

"I know what he did," responded Pepper. You don't have to remind me that he moved Ian in with him. But I was sick back then. I wasn't myself. As much as I hate to admit it, Ian *did* help Xavier with the boys. I won't deny that. But when I got better and I told him I wanted to come home, what did he do? He called off the divorce, told Ian it was over, and welcomed me back home. I know that was hard on him; I'm not saying it wasn't. But he had a family, Eliana. Gay or not, I'm his wife. He owed it to me and his sons to try to make things work. And he still does."

"Girl, don't you see, the man *has* tried. He's tried to make it work for the past three years! It's obvious he couldn't keep up the charade or else he'd still be here. His heart wasn't in it and now look, he's gone. He left you, his sons, and everything connected to his life. Why do you think he did that, Pepper? Please, wake up already!"

Pepper remained quiet like she was in deep thought. She shrugged. "I...I don't know what to think, what to feel, or how to act anymore. I'm so confused. All I wanted was to be happy, to have a family, a good man by my side, someone who was different from my daddy. Don't get me wrong, after their divorce, my father always provided for me financially, but to this day, I rarely talk to him and when I do, it's like he's always busy doing something. He recently got married again, for the third time. This time to some filthy rich chick. He's somewhere living his best life in Costa Rica. He hasn't even met his grandkids in person. Only seen them on video chat, or through pictures I post or send him."

"Look, you have to let your father do what's best for him, and you, my friend, it's time to focus on you. Learn how to love yourself, Pepper. You have a lot to offer and a lot of love to give. You have those two beautiful boys who need you. You can't let Xavier send you down another slippery slope. You can't do it, Pepper."

twelve

"I'm exhausted from trying to be stronger than I feel."
Unknown

Xavier swiftly unlocked the door to his Airbnb and made a beeline for the bathroom. He had spent most of the afternoon, and into the evening, people-watching in the massive park along the Willamette River.

After relieving himself, he turned on the shower while he undressed. Immersing himself under the hot jet streams of the rain shower, he could feel the water melting away his stress. While under the shower spray, he realized he had been away from his family and home for going on a month, still with no clear plan of when he would return.

When he was finished with his shower, he put on a fresh pair of boxer briefs, went into the kitchen, and prepared a mediocre microwave dinner. While munching on the lackluster food, he daydreamed about his mother's mouthwatering deep-dish spinach and broccoli quiche. With a pang of homesickness, he retreated to his bedroom, grabbed his burner phone, and contemplated calling Fancy but ultimately decided to send her a text instead.

"Hi, Mom. It's Xavier. Just want u to know I'm good. don't worry about me. Just keep me uplifted in prayer. Not sure when I'll be back so if you don't mind, please help Pepper with the boys. do not try to call me back. You will not be able to

reach me. love you. Xavier." He pressed
SEND and then returned the phone to the night
table before going back to the kitchen to finish his
meal.

Next, Xavier pulled out a pint of vodka he had
purchased earlier and took a swig straight from the
bottle. Drinking had become his new routine of
late. Almost every night and sometimes during the
day, he would have a few shots or more to calm his
mind. He frowned at his growing dependence but
ultimately downed the bottle of alcohol.

He staggered to the balcony, gazing up at the
starry sky before uttering a desperate prayer,
slurring his words in his inebriated state. "God, I
need you. Why have you turned your back on me?"
he murmured, starting to sway unsteadily. "I don't
know how much longer I can fight against this war
between my flesh and mind," he wept.

†

Pepper finished bathing the boys and put them
to bed before indulging in a bath and then settling
into her empty king-sized bed. She curled up with
a book she had been reading for the past month,
attempting to relax. Normally, a book of this length
would take her a day, two at the most, but lately,
she found it difficult to focus and keep her
thoughts clear. She missed Xavier terribly. She
wished she hadn't insisted that her mother and
Fancy leave her home alone. The truth of the
matter was if one, or both of them, were at her
house, she wouldn't feel so lonely and isolated.

She struggled to keep depressive thoughts at
bay. Unable to concentrate, she rose from the bed,

shuffled to the kitchen, and made herself a cup of hot chocolate, settling at the island. However, her thoughts soon overwhelmed her, and she broke down in tears. For what seemed like the hundredth time, she looked at the number Xavier had called from. When she tried to call him back, it was clear that he had used a fake number to make a spoof call, and she couldn't trace it.

The last communication she received from him was a brief text saying the same thing he'd said before. "I'm fine. Do not worry. Take care. Zay." There was no mention of her, the boys, or their well-being, leaving Pepper in a state of more uncertainty about his welfare.

She thought about what Eliana had said. Had she only been attracted to Xavier because he was nice and kind and treated her like she wanted a man to treat her? What was wrong with her? What could have possessed her to marry a gay man? Could she really have low self-esteem?

Raising the mug to her lips, hoping to relish the rich and flavorful taste of the piping-hot chocolate, the now lukewarm and unappetizing liquid only added to her growing frustration. Her mind became consumed with relentless thoughts that eventually led her to pound the sturdy marble counter with a tightly clenched fist, unleashing a torrent of anger and frustration over the current state of her life.

thirteen

*"Breaking up is like a mirror, it's better to leave it
broken than to hurt yourself trying to fix it."*
Unknown

Xavier stirred from his slumber and rubbed his
eyes before glancing at the clock on the night table.
"SUN 9:55". In Memphis, Sunday mornings were
reserved for attending New Holy Rock with Pepper
and their boys. But instead of enjoying service with
his wife, Xavier was usually locked away in the
church's finance room, tallying the donations from
Sunday service.

Without hesitation, he rose from the bed and
headed for the shower. Once finished, he flipped
through the meager selection of clothing he had
packed and settled on a pair of tan slacks and a
polo shirt.

After grooming himself, Xavier stepped out of
the Airbnb and started strolling up the street.
Although he hadn't noticed many churches in the
area where he was staying, today he was
determined to find a place where he could hear a
message from God. Maybe it would help lighten the
feeling of despair forming heavily around his heart.

Fortunately, the efficient transit system made it
a breeze to get around the city, a welcome change
from his usual reliance on a car. Boarding the first
bus that arrived, he admired the picturesque
greenery zipping by outside the window.

Caught up in his thoughts and the passing
scenery, he checked his phone and realized he had
lost track of time.

Exiting the bus at the next stop, he noticed people entering a nearby church and decided to follow. Taking a seat at the back of the sanctuary, he waited for the service to start.

Within minutes, Xavier was delighted to witness a diverse choir of approximately thirty casually dressed individuals assembling in the choir stand. When they began singing, their voices blended seamlessly in perfect harmony, filling the small sanctuary with a powerful sense of worship and praise.

Xavier's spirit was soon stirred and he found himself fully immersed in the joyful atmosphere. With unrestrained enthusiasm, he clapped his hands as if he had not a single care or concern in the world.

✝

After Sunday service Stiles, Victoria, and Fancy gathered for a late lunch. Fancy brought Zavion and Davion along, having picked them up the night before so the boys could spend the night with her and Pepper could get some rest.

"I've had everybody I know to see what they could find out," Fancy offered, eyeing her grandsons while they sat contentedly eating their plates of mac 'n cheese with chicken strips. "I'm so worried. Where is he?" she said, fighting back tears. "I was glad to get a text from him again, but truthfully it only caused me to worry even more. He said he was okay, but I don't believe it. I know my sons. Xavier is going through something heavy and I'm afraid that the end result may not be good."

"If you don't mind, let me see the text again," Stiles said.

"I don't mind. Here you go."

Stiles read the text. "And we can't reach him on this number?"

"Nope," said Victoria. "I think he's calling from a spoof app or something like that. That's what Pepper thinks, and I agree." She wiped the mouths of one of the boys. "At least he's communicated with the two of you."

"I guess," said Fancy, sighing.

Stiles passed the phone back to Fancy. "I say we just keep his name before the Lord. That's all we can do."

"You're right. Prayer is the key, but still what puzzles me is the Xavier I've come to know has always been caring and he loves these boys," Victoria said.

Stiles looked at the boys and smiled.

"Which is why for the life of me, I can't understand why he would take off and not let anyone know where he is. I don't like it," Victoria complained.

"If Hezekiah was out of prison, he would have found him by now. I just know it," boasted Fancy.

"Speaking of my brother, his lawyer should be hearing from the appeals board soon. God knows I'm praying that Hezekiah will be set free. From what Christian Black says, there's more than a good chance for a turnover of his conviction. It just takes time. As for me, you, and all of us," Stiles said, looking at Victoria and Fancy, we have to stick together, be strong for Pepper and the boys, and wait patiently as we can for God to do what He does best and that's work things out for our good."

"Does Hezekiah know about Xavier? Has anyone told him?" Victoria eyed Fancy and then Stiles.

"No, not yet, I plan to drive up there this week and tell him. I was hoping I wouldn't have to. The man has had his share of bad news lately, especially with what took place at New Holy Rock, not to mention what happened to Christian Black's wife. That could easily have set things back since Black had to take some time off."

"Oh, yes, that was terrible," said Fancy.

"It sure was," Victoria agreed.

"But the good thing is she's going to be okay," said Stiles. "God protected that woman."

Victoria and Fancy nodded.

"I also held off telling Hezekiah about Xavier because I was sure Xavier would have returned by now and I wouldn't have to dump this load on my brother," Stiles said, shaking his head, and wiping his mouth with his cloth napkin.

"You already know he's not going to take the news well," Fancy said, taking a bite of her food. "Especially when he finds out it's been over a month, thirty-two days today to be exact since Xavier left."

"I understand that, but Hezekiah knows, just like we all do, that at the end of the day, we have to remain faithful. We must believe that God has Xavier covered. He knows what we're going through and he's already making a way out of no way."

"I'm glad you feel that way, but why wouldn't you? You work for God. Your faith is limitless," Victoria added and lightly chuckled.

Stiles shook his head. "Not by a long shot. I still have moments when I question God's ways and His timing. I'm not perfect. None of us are. I just try to operate from a place of blind faith. God says for us to receive we have to believe first. Now, enough of the preaching. I've done enough of that for the day. Let's concentrate on this delicious food before us," he said, eyeing the loaded table.

fourteen

"Depression is a prison where you are both the suffering prisoner and the cruel jailer." D. Rowe

After leaving the church, Xavier took a stroll through the neighborhood until he stumbled upon a charming Mediterranean restaurant. The inviting menu convinced him to treat himself to a meal, and he allowed the courteous hostess to lead him to his seat.

While savoring his food, snippets of the minister's sermon replayed in his head. One particular part of the message resonated with him: *He knows everything about you. He knows all the sins you've committed, will commit, and are committing. You may be able to hide the real you from the world, but you can't hide from God.* The meaning of this message slowly consumed him, and a shroud of depressing thoughts saturated his mind.

With each bite, his appetite dwindled as he was overwhelmed by the weight of his actions. Eventually, he signaled for a to-go box, eager to retreat to his Airbnb.

Sitting on the bus his mind was still plagued by the preacher's words. *Although God knows everything about you, He still loves you.* It had definitely struck a chord, reminding him that although one may conceal their true self from other people, there is no hiding from the all-seeing eye of God.

His mind troubled, instead of proceeding to his Airbnb, he stopped again, this time at one of the local bars where he had a couple of shots of vodka. He dismissed the obvious fact it was not quite afternoon, a little early to start drinking. And it was a Sunday. Shortly after arriving, and without thinking or considering any repercussions of his decisions or the thoughts that had just wracked his mind, Xavier found himself sitting at a table, talking, laughing, and drinking with three strange men.

He must have agreed to go with them back to their place because he woke up hours later in a strange house surrounded by unfamiliar faces and half-naked men. This was too much for his mind to process. How could he have repeated the same stupid, careless behavior? What was wrong with him?

He sat upright on the sofa and looked around, again not knowing where he was. This was like a repeat of the night he brought the Connor fellow to his hotel suite. Only this time, he was not at a hotel or his Airbnb, but someplace totally unfamiliar.

Xavier was afraid, and his heart began racing when he saw a naked man lying on the couch opposite where he had been sleeping. *Oh my, God!* Suppose the sleeping man was dangerous, a serial killer or murderer? His mind raced with wild and scary thoughts. He made sure he was careful not to wake him while he scanned the room for his clothes. He saw his pants nearby, grabbed them, and quietly put them on.

Next, he eased through the house to find his shirt and shoes. He came upon a bedroom and looked inside. No one was in there. He walked further up the hallway, arriving at another bedroom. In this bedroom was another guy sprawled across the bed naked with drug paraphernalia lying on the table next to him. A half-empty liquor bottle lay on the floor near where Xavier spotted his shirt and loafers.

He lingered in the bedroom doorway for a few seconds before he carefully walked across the carpeted floor, grabbed his shirt and shoes, and then turned around slowly, making his way up the hallway until he saw the front door. He rushed outside while putting on his shirt and stepping into his shoes.

The burst of fresh air welcomed his face, and he exhaled, thankful to have gotten out of that place without incident. *Thank you, Lord. Thank you for rescuing me again.*

Xavier set out walking, still not sure exactly where he was. He looked at his phone. It was past midnight. As he approached a nearby street sign and intersection, he began to gather his sense of direction and an hour later he was walking into his townhome Airbnb.

While he took a shower, he began to recall in bits and pieces some of what happened between him and the strange men. It sickened him to the point he rushed out of the shower and puked, the vile vomit barely landing in the toilet. He thought of himself as a terrible, terrible human being. He burst into tears as he fell to his knees and onto the cold tile floor, pleading and crying out to God to help him.

fifteen

"I am in that temper that if I were under water I would scarcely kick to come to the top." John Keats

Xavier was consumed with self-blame for his actions and felt dejected and hopeless as he wandered around the Airbnb. He needed something to take the edge off, to calm down his thoughts. He went into the kitchen and got the unopened bottle of vodka. He didn't bother getting a glass, but opened the bottle and took a giant gulp.

What in the heck was wrong with him? Why was he suddenly displaying such stupid behavior? He needed someone to talk to, someone who would listen, who understood him. There was only one person he could think of: Ian Hodges. But Ian was a thing of the past.

The more he drank, the more he dwelled on his traumatic past, criticizing himself for his sexual orientation and his perceived weaknesses. Did he have no moral character? He thought about how nasty and sinful his actions had been with the strangers he'd slept with during the short time he'd been in Portland. What kind of person was he? He had committed horrible, shameless, adulterous acts, not with women, but with men. What if they transmitted an STD or worse? He felt like such a failure, at least that's how his actions made him feel.

He burst into tears as the barrage of memories started racing through his mind. His worst memory was that of being molested at the age of nine by an older teen boy who lived in their neighborhood. He had kept it a secret for all these years. He often thought that being molested was the reason he was gay. He wasn't sure; he didn't know what to think. What he did know was that being molested, in and of itself, kept him in a mental state of fear and inward anger. He always felt like it had been his fault, although he was just a kid at the time.

He wished he had confided in someone about what happened back then, but he never could bring himself to tell his religious, sometimes judgmental, condemning parents, especially his father.

When he became a teen and his parents learned he was gay, they did not hide their feelings about it. It was an abomination, a sin, and downright shame, they told him. They told him he was going against God's teaching. Even Khalil didn't want to be around him. This made matters worse as he grew up and became a young man.

And then there was Leo, a deacon at Holy Rock and his uncle Stiles's best friend. He didn't wish harm, let alone death on anyone, but the day he learned Leo had been murdered, he felt such relief. Leo reminded him of when he was molested. Leo had touched him inappropriately like he had permission and the right to do so. He had humiliated him and made him relive when he was a frightened nine-year-old boy with nowhere to turn and no one to help him. So, yes, when Leo was found murdered, Xavier felt like vengeance had been carried out on his behalf.

More thoughts raced through his mind. He had another shot of vodka. He mumbled incoherently while calling out the name of his first love, Raymone. Xavier and Raymone were teenagers when they met and became a secret couple. He shed fresh tears when he realized it was because of him that Raymone was a paraplegic. All because of a car accident that was Xavier's fault.

Xavier continued his self-attacks. With each horrid memory that resurfaced, he took another drink. Moping around the townhome, he beat up on himself for being such a hypocrite. On the one hand, he was supposed to be a Christian man, a godly person, but how could he call himself a Christian when he was desiring and sleeping with men?

Then there was his wife and sons, his mother, and his brother. Speaking on his brother, why wasn't he more like Khalil? Khalil was confident, assertive, and aggressive. A ladies' man at that. He went after what he wanted without caring if he hurt someone along the way. Khalil was not one to be pushed into doing something he did not want to do. He could be kind but tough. Khalil could cuss you out without cussing. Yes, Khalil was more like their father than Xavier ever would be.

Consumed with so many conflicting thoughts Xavier took another swig and went and stood out on the balcony, looking up at the starless sky. The more he consumed the alcohol the more his mind played over his past like a fine-tuned piano until he was in a drunken stupor, wrestling his past and chastising himself for being such a horrible person,

56

a terrible father, a lying hypocrite, and a cheating husband. It had to stop. He had to do something or else he would ruin the lives of his sons, and God only knows how many other people, including Pepper. He didn't want to do that. He couldn't do that. He wouldn't do that. It was at that very moment, Xavier knew exactly what it was he had to do.

sixteen

"A marriage without love is like a house without a foundation, destined to crumble." Unknown

Pepper's concern for her husband increasingly grew. Despite the best efforts of Fancy and Khalil, no one had been able to locate him. This was day forty of his absence, and the sixth day since she last received a text. Pepper woke up feeling weighed down by the uncertainty of it all. Zavion and Davion's high energy only added to her discombobulated state. She had made the tough decision days before to let the nanny go for financial reasons. There was still ample money in their bank accounts, but she had no idea when Xavier would return so she thought it best to spend and budget more carefully. She remained thankful for Victoria and Fancy. They were a constant source of support checking on her and the kids daily.

Another source of support came in the form of Rolonda, a former co-worker and friend. The two met at work a few years prior to Pepper meeting Xavier. They instantly connected and formed a strong friendship. But life happened, and their friendship took a hit when Rolonda's husband was transferred to Utah. Over time, communication between the friends weakened before stopping altogether.

A recent chance encounter at Wal-Mart brought them back together.

"How long since you moved back to Memphis?" Pepper asked as the ladies caught up on each other's lives.

"It's been a month."

"Where are y'all living?"

"We were lucky, girl. We were able to move back into our old house. The timing couldn't have been more perfect. Our tenant's lease was coming to an end around the same time we got news of Drake being transferred back to Memphis."

"That was a blessing," Pepper replied.

"It sure was. We didn't have to do much fixing up either. Thank God, the tenant maintained it well. What about you? How are Xavier and the boys?"

Pepper opened up about the difficulties in her marriage. It was as if a dam burst and Pepper couldn't hold back expressing her emotions. Being able to be open and vulnerable was one of the things she had missed most about her friendship with Rolonda. She shared the painful truth about Xavier's infidelity, about him leaving, and the toll it had taken on her and their family.

When Pepper initially told Rolonda that she had fallen for this great guy who happened to be gay, Rolonda warned her that Xavier was not the right one. Despite the warning, Pepper pursued the relationship and here she was three years later, miserable, lost, and alone. In hindsight, she realized Rolonda had been right all along.

After an hour-long catchup session in the store aisles, the friends exchanged numbers and promised to maintain contact.

†

As Pepper attempted to juggle her incessant thoughts with her sons clamoring for cookies and juice, the sound of the doorbell disrupted her rhythm. She paused, briefly considering whether to answer it, her eyes flickering over to her boys as she urged them to tidy up their toys if they wanted a treat.

Approaching the front door, she could see through the frosted glass silhouettes of two people, one appearing to be a woman and the other a man. When she opened the door, she saw two police officers. This couldn't be good news. Suddenly, she felt a round of nausea overtake her, and she leaned against the door frame, just to make sure she wouldn't fall.

"Can I help you?" she asked, holding her quivering belly and trying to keep her voice steady, despite her growing anxiety.

"Are you okay, ma'am?" the female officer asked, taking a step forward.

"Yes, I'm...fine," Pepper whispered. "This is about my husband, isn't it?"

The tall, dark-haired officer introduced himself and asked if they could come inside. Pepper's heart raced as she tried to process what was happening. It was as if she had been sucked into a vacuum. She couldn't comprehend what was being said. Her thoughts went all over the place. Had something happened to Xavier? Was he in trouble? She tried to remain calm as she led the officers to the family room, where her sons were now bickering with each other over toys.

"Pipe down. Pick up those toys like I told you or no treats. I mean it," she demanded.

The boys continued whining but they began picking up their toys.

"We need to ask you a few questions about your husband, Xavier McCoy," one of them said, taking a seat across from her.

Pepper felt her hands start to shake as the female officer explained that a male fitting Xavier's description had been found deceased in Portland, Oregon. As the officers continued to speak, Pepper felt her heart drop into her stomach. The news hit her like a ton of bricks, and she couldn't believe what she was hearing. *Xavier? Deceased? Dead? No way. There had to be some kind of mistake.*

She felt tears welling up in her eyes as she listened to the male officer. "Your husband was staying at an Airbnb in Portland, Oregon. It appears," he paused before saying, "he jumped or fell from his tenth-floor balcony. I hate to tell you this, Mrs. McCoy, but we strongly believe from the information we received from the PPD, that your husband committed suicide."

"Suicide? No way," Pepper lashed out. "Xavier would never do something like that. He would never leave his boys," she said, looking teary-eyed at her sons playing with their toys instead of picking them up.

"I know it may be hard to believe, but alongside several empty liquor bottles, a note was found inside the townhome, indicating that he had been deeply depressed and he didn't want to burden his family anymore. I'm sorry."

Pepper felt like the wind had been knocked out of her. She knew Xavier struggled with depression from time to time, but not to this extent. Why didn't he talk to her? Why would he do something like this? She sobbed into her hands, while the boys ran up to her, not knowing or understanding why their mommy was crying.

The female officer reached out and put a comforting hand on her shoulder. "We're sorry for your loss, Mrs. McCoy. Is there anyone we can call for you?"

Pepper, like a robot, slowly shook her head. At that moment, she went numb. She couldn't believe that Xavier was gone, that she would never see him again. Her mind raced as she thought about how she was going to tell their children, and how she was going to deal with the aftermath of his death. A death by suicide.

The officers stayed with her for a little while longer, answering her questions and offering condolences. Pepper appreciated their kindness, but all she wanted was to be alone to process what was happening.

After the officers left, she sat on the couch staring at the wall, trying to make sense of what they had told her. This was all so unreal. It had to be some kind of a nightmare, anything other than reality. She couldn't imagine a world without Xavier, and she didn't know how she was going to move forward.

seventeen

"The only way to get through grief is to go through it." Robert Frost

The next few days as Pepper tried to accept Xavier's death, she found a bit of consolation in talking about it with Khalil. Khalil opened up about his own struggles with grief and guilt.

"I should have been there for him," Khalil said, his voice heavy with emotion. "I knew he was having a hard time coping with his sexuality, but dang, I didn't know he was thinking about taking himself out. I should have been a better brother. I should have seen that he was hurting."

Pepper put a hand on Khalil's shoulder. "It's not your fault. Xavier was dealing with a lot, and he didn't reach out to any of us for help. It's not anyone's fault."

Khalil nodded, but Pepper could see the pain in his eyes.

"What about my father? Do you know if anyone has spoken to him?" he asked.

"Yes, Stiles told him over the phone, which he hated to do. But Hezekiah had already seen it on the news. Of course, the man is beyond devastated," Pepper said, her voice soft and tearful. "He's already called twice today to check on me and the kids."

During their conversation, Fancy arrived. Khalil rose from the porch and approached his mother, hugging her and planting a kiss on her cheek. He took hold of her hand and led her to the expansive front porch, where they settled on the steps.

"He was my baby, my baby boy," Fancy cried, her voice barely audible through her sobs. "Why, oh, God! Why?"

Khalil wrapped his arms around her. There was nothing he could say to make the pain go away. He hoped that his presence would provide a bit of comfort.

"I can't believe my baby's gone," Fancy continued crying, her voice shaking. "I keep thinking it's all a bad dream."

Pepper could see the grief etched on her mother-in-law's face and tears pricked at the corners of her own eyes. She understood Fancy's pain. She felt the same agony of grief. "We'll get through this together. We have to, for the boys," she told Fancy.

It wasn't going to be easy, but Pepper knew at that moment that she had to be strong for her children, herself, and her family. She had to figure out how to raise two toddlers on her own while dealing with her own grief and the grief of those around her. It was a heavy burden, but she had to keep going for the sake of her children and for Xavier's memory.

†

Hezekiah's world was shattered when he heard the news of Xavier's death, hitting him like a ton of bricks, leaving him a broken man behind bars. He was consumed by a range of emotions - despair, rage, and hopelessness - as he struggled to come to terms with his devastating loss.

†

The day before Xavier's funeral, Hezekiah was driven by prison van and escorted by correction officers to Memphis where he was permitted to view his son's body. However, even amid this heart-wrenching moment, Hezekiah was bound by handcuffs and shackles, a cruel and constant reminder of his imprisonment and helplessness.

Standing alone in front of his son's casket, heavy tears ran down his face, each one carrying with it a lifetime of regret and sorrow. Hezekiah was consumed by thoughts of what he could have done differently, what words he could have said to prevent Xavier from choosing such a tragic end. He clung to memories of his son, the good and the bad while the pain of the present moment washed over him like a tidal wave. The weight of his guilt was almost too much to bear as he struggled to come to terms with the loss of his beloved Xavier.

eighteen

"You don't get over it, you just get through it."
Wendy Feireisen

The funeral was a blur, with friends and family offering condolences and sharing fond memories of Xavier. Pepper felt like a shell of herself, going through the motions without really feeling anything.

Several days after the funeral she received a FedEx envelope from a person who identified himself as a licensed therapist—a Dr. Henry Lewis. Pepper had no idea Xavier had been seeing a therapist. She knew he fought the demons of his sexuality, but he never told her about Dr. Lewis.

In the letter, Dr. Lewis explained that before Xavier left Memphis, he had been counseling Xavier professionally for several months. According to him, Xavier had been struggling with bouts of severe depression for quite some time. Dr. Lewis had been trying to get Xavier to seek additional help, including hospitalization and medication, but Xavier had refused, believing that he could handle his demons. Unfortunately, he couldn't.

As she read the letter, her emotions started to get the best of her, and an indescribable sense of sorrow began to overtake her. Initially, anger surged through her veins, directed at Xavier for abandoning their children and leaving them fatherless. Yet, deep within her soul, she couldn't help but ponder if she could have done more to help him.

Pepper's mind was haunted by *what-ifs* that now seemed to mock her, taunting her with thoughts of how things could have been different. If only she had been able to recognize the extent of Xavier's struggles, perhaps she could have been there for him in his darkest moments—like he had tried to be there for her.

Why had she been so set on being part of his life in the first place? Why did she push her way of life onto him? Why hadn't she listened when Rolonda warned her from the very beginning that she was making a mistake by fooling around with a gay man? Why? And now this. Xavier was gone. He was so miserable that he felt his life was not worth continuing.

Tears stung her eyes as she grappled with the harsh reality of her loss. She never imagined that Xavier would choose to leave them all behind in this way. She couldn't help but think about all the times she had thought about reaching out to him, but held back, afraid of stirring up old memories and reopening old wounds, plus she had her own mental health to protect. She never wanted to go back to that dark place she'd gone to after she had her babies. She questioned herself incessantly, wondering if her presence in his life had made it worse. If only she had given him more space to live the life he desired, perhaps things would have been different.

Clutching the letter close to her chest, Pepper's heart throbbed with a sense of loss. Her dream of living happily ever after with Xavier and the boys was clearly not to be. The words in the letter echoed in her mind, a reminder of the fleeting nature of life and the importance of cherishing every moment with those we love. At that moment, Pepper vowed to honor Xavier's memory by teaching her sons about the good man their father was, sharing stories of his love, kindness, and laughter. She would hold on to every laugh they shared and every precious moment they spent together. The road ahead was uncertain, but she knew that honoring Xavier's memory would be a source of comfort and strength, a reminder to embrace every moment with the ones we love and never take a single day for granted.

nineteen

"It doesn't get better, it just gets different." Feireisen

As the days trickled past, Pepper sought solace in her children and threw herself into being the best mother she could be. She knew that Xavier would have wanted her to take care of the boys, and she made it her mission to give them the love and support they needed. Fancy, Hezekiah, and Khalil struggled to cope with their loss in their own ways.

Fancy was consumed by grief, her heart shattered by the loss of her son. She struggled to find if there was still meaning in life without her beloved baby boy. She had visited his grave every day since his death, talking to him as if he were still there. She hoped to find some comfort in knowing that he was finally at peace.

Hezekiah struggled with the guilt of not being there for his son when he needed him the most. How he wished he could turn back time. He would be a better father. He projected his sorrow and pain through writing, keeping notes in a notepad he purchased from the commissary. He wrote letters to Pepper and his grandchildren, expressing his love and regret for not being there for them but promising that when he was released he would make it up to them.

Khalil found it difficult to come to terms with the fact that his brother was gone. He regretted that he and Xavier were never close. He felt like he had failed him as an older brother. He could see that now. He could never accept his little brother for who he was and Xavier never felt comfortable being himself around Khalil. Could their relationship have been different if he had tried harder to connect with him? He found himself lost in thought, trying to make sense of what had happened. Why did Xavier take his life? Okay, so Xavier was gay, but did that warrant him committing suicide? Khalil had a hard time grasping that explanation. But Khalil realized that he couldn't change the past and the best thing he could do was to honor Xavier's memory by being a better brother to Xavier in death than he had been in life.

He would make an effort to connect more with his family, particularly his nephews, and to be there for them when they needed him, including being a father figure for them in place of his brother. It may be too little too late, but still, Khalil promised God and Xavier he would give it his best shot.

Stiles was the pillar of strength the family needed, having already endured his own personal journey through grief many times in his life. The loss of his beloved mother Audrey, his biological mother Margaret, his one and only sister, Francesca, and the ultimate pain—the tragic death of his little girl.

Now, grief had visited his doorstep yet again. But with a strong, unwavering faith in God, Stiles called upon God for strength. He prayed that his family would also find the strength to endure the loss of someone so dear. Stiles understood death was inevitable. He knew, personally, the trail of hurt and pain it leaves behind can be indescribable. His friend and fellow online instructor, Mya, had been there for him in ways he did not expect. He was grateful for her presence, as it helped ease some of his pain.

In the end, despite their ongoing journeys of healing and recovery, this family understood that more challenges would likely come, and their futures remained uncertain. Nonetheless, a bit of peace was found in knowing they could face any challenges that came their way together, as a family, relying on each other for support, drawing strength from the memory of Xavier.

Xavier's death might very well pave the way for reconciliation. Through his death, Stiles prayed the family would be set free. It had taken years for him to forgive himself, and others. The fact he could not forgive others was like walking around in a mental state of unhappiness, even as a man of God. Stiles wanted his family to not allow Xavier's death to separate them but to connect them because Xavier was finally free.

Stiles stood with his family, each of them holding hands as they gathered around the dinner table. Next to him stood Pepper and Xavier's two boys. Stiles moved his hand from Pepper's and wrapped it around her shoulder.

He prayed, "Lord, God, forgive us. Set us free from guilt and self-condemnation. Remind us that through *You* we can be set free. We can be set free from our mistakes, from all the mess-ups and hiccups that life sporadically and unexpectedly spreads across our lives. We can be set free...for whom the son sets free is free indeed!"

WORDS FROM THE AUTHOR

Xavier McCoy struggled with loving himself and seeing himself the way God sees each of us. God looks on our hearts. He knows us inside and out. Yes, we all have imperfections and challenges, and none of us is perfect, yet God loves us—still. Xavier could not and would not accept the person he was. He did not realize despite his fleshly desires and all of his sinful shortcomings, he was loved by God with unconditional love. Xavier sunk into a deep pit of depression, and he could never seem to fully climb out of it. Unfortunately, he chose to take matters into his own hands and appoint himself as his own judge, juror, and executioner. That is never a good choice.

If you are battling depression, have suicidal thoughts, and/or feelings of hopelessness, I employ you to reach *up* to God and reach *out* to others for help and healing.

Be encouraged. I hope you enjoy reading my work and I thank you for traveling this literary journey along with me. Until the next perfect story about imperfect people like you....and me!

Continue reading about this family in the next installment of the "My Son's Wife" series, coming soon to your favorite book retailer.

More Perfect Stories About Imperfect People Like
You...and Me

MY SON'S WIFE SERIES
My Son's Wife: The Beginning (Book 1)
My Son's Ex-Wife: Aftershock (Book 2)
My Son's Next Wife (Book 3)
My Sister My Momma My Wife (Book 4)
My Wife My Baby...And Him (Book 5)
The McCoys of Holy Rock (Book 6)
Dem McCoy Boys (Book 7)
My Brother, Father...And Me (Book 8)
My Truth, My Time, My Turn (Book 9)
Dem Folk at Holy Rock (Book 10)
Thicker Than Water (Book 11)
Redeeming Holy Rock (12)
**This series is continuing

HOLY ROCK CHRONICLES
(MY SON'S WIFE SHORT STORY SPIN-OFF)
Calling Dr. Daniels
The Woman in Apartment 3D
Ruthless Rianna

Christian Black, Esq.
If Your Price Is Right
Love Shoulda Brought You Home

ADVERSE CITY SERIES
The Real Housewives of Adverse City 1
The Real Housewives of Adverse City 2
The Real Housewives of Adverse City 3
The Real Housewives of Adverse City 4

CONTACT INFORMATION

www.sheliaebell.net
www.sheliawritesbooks.com
sheliawritesbooks@yahoo.com
www.facebook.com/sheliawritesbooks
@sheliaebell (Twitter & Instagram)

Please join my mailing list
for literary updates and new book release
information
www.sheliawritesbooks.com

If you enjoyed this book or any of my books, please
go to your favorite review site and leave a positive
review!

Other links to my books
bit.ly/sheliaebell
bit.ly/sheliabn
bit.ly/sheliabell

www.sheliawritesbooks.com

#iwriteforfilmandtv
#iwritebestsellers
#iwritepageturners
#iwritenewyorktimesbestsellers
#iamgodsamazinggirl

Perfect Stories About Imperfect People Like You
...and Me!

www.ingramcontent.com/pod-product-compliance
Lightning Source LLC
Chambersburg PA
CBHW051313170626
46809CB00004B/1883